D1515922

TITCHY WITCH
and the
Frog Fiasco

For Kaia
R.I.

For Daisy and Owen
K.M.

Orchard Books
96 Leonard Street, London EC2A 4XD
Orchard Books Australia
32/45-51 Huntley Street, Alexandria, NSW 2015
First published in Great Britain in 2003
First paperback publication 2004
ISBN 1 84121 046 3 (HB)
ISBN 1 84121 122 2 (PB)

Text © Rose Impey 2003 Illustrations © Katharine McEwen 2003
The rights of Rose Impey to be identified as the author and
Katharine McEwen to be identified as the illustrator of this Work
have been asserted by them in accordance with the
Copyright, Designs and Patents Act, 1988.
A CIP catalogue record for this book is available from the British Library
1 3 5 7 9 10 8 6 4 2 (HB)
3 5 7 9 10 8 6 4 (PB)
Printed in Hong Kong

TITCHY WITCH

and the

Frog Fiasco

Rose Impey ★ Katharine McEwen

ORCHARD BOOKS

Titchy-witch

Victor

Eric

Wendel

Weeny-witch

Witchy-witch

Cat-a-bogus

Titchy-witch was always
in trouble with her teacher.
Miss Foulbreath was a real ogre.

It didn't seem fair.
Miss Foulbreath never saw
Primrose looking
at herself in
a mirror.

And she never saw Gobby-goblin, poking people with his poky little finger.

But she *always* saw Titchy-witch poking him back.

The next time Gobby-goblin poked
her, Titchy-witch put a spell
on him.

The spots didn't last long.

But Titchy-witch had to write
one hundred times: *I must not
do magic at school.*

Titchy-witch told Cat-a-bogus, "I don't want to go to school any more."

"Little witches have to go to school," the cat growled, "to learn to read spells."

"I can read," said Titchy-witch.

"Hmmm," purred the cat.

"We'll see about that."

"What does this say?" he asked.
Titchy-witch couldn't read
long words yet, but she had a go.
"Dis-dis...Dizzy Potion?"
she said, hopefully.

The cat rolled his eyes.
"I think somebody needs
to do some homework."

"I *can* read," Titchy-witch told Dido. "I could read spells, if I wanted to."

Titchy-witch lifted down her
mum's Big Book of Spells.
Just to have a look.

Uh, oh!

15

Oh, yes! Titchy-witch had always wanted to turn a prince into a frog.

How to Turn a Prince Into a Frog...

fig.1

Trouble was she didn't have a
prince right now. "Don't worry,
Victor," said Titchy-witch.
"Spells are easy-breezy."

How to Turn a
Prince Into a
Frog...

But this one wasn't.

Titchy-witch didn't get it all wrong.

Just bits of it.

"Turn this vulture into a...frog.
I mean prince!"
There was a *flash!*
and a *crash!*

Titchy-witch was very pleased with herself. The frog wasn't so pleased.

Cro-o-ak!

"Don't worry, Victor," she said, patting his head. "We'll soon have you back."

But then...

...the fat little frog turned into two fat little frogs. Then four, then eight... In no time at all, the kitchen was full of frogs.

Titchy-witch tried to sweep them outside.

But the more she swept, the more frogs appeared.

Titchy-witch didn't know what to do next.

The frogs made so much noise,
they woke Cat-a-bogus.

ribbit

The cat didn't like being
woken up.

It all went
wrong

"I think someone had better learn to read before she does any more magic," he growled. "Or she could be in *big* trouble!"

With a twitch of his tail and
a waggle of his whiskers,
the cat did a little magic
of his own.

"Up-sy, down-sy,
round as well,
widdershins-wise,
undo this spell."

In a flash Victor was back.
And all the frogs had disappeared.
Well, almost all of them.

When Mum and Dad came in to say goodnight, Titchy-witch was reading the *Little Witch's First Book of Spells.*

"How was school today?" they asked.

Titchy-witch smiled.
"I think it will be better tomorrow,"
she said.

TITCHY WITCH

Rose Impey ★ Katharine McEwen

Enjoy a little more magic with all the Titchy-witch tales:

All priced at £4.99 each

Colour Crunchies are available from all good
bookshops, or can be ordered direct from the publisher:
Orchard Books, PO BOX 29, Douglas IM99 1BQ
Credit card orders please telephone 01624 836000
or fax 01624 837033
or e-mail: bookshop@enterprise.net for details.

To order please quote title, author and ISBN
and your full name and address.
Cheques and postal orders should be
made payable to 'Bookpost plc'.
Postage and packing is FREE within the UK
(overseas customers should add £1.00 per book).

Prices and availability are subject to change.